Ag Medical Advice

RUTH ANNA EVANS

Copyright © 2024 by Ruth Anna Evans

All rights reserved.

No portion of this book may be reproduced in any form without written permission from the publisher or author, except as permitted by U.S. copyright law.

To the parents of medically fragile children.
My heart is with you.

To those social workers who deal with impossible
sadness with kindness and compassion every day.
You are heroes.

Chapter One

"Daddy, I don't feel good." Maddie rubbed the sleep from her eyes, which were heavy with dark circles in her pale little face. Frank brushed aside her dark hair and laid his hand on her forehead. It was cool and dry. But he believed her. Usually she popped out of bed in the morning, following him around the house telling her little jokes while he tried to convince her to brush her teeth.

"You have school, little Froggie, what's wrong?"

"My stomach hurts, and it feels hard to breathe."

That was a new one to Frank. He wished Tisha wasn't on that cruise. He didn't regret encouraging her to go, but he missed her in little moments like these. It was a once-in-a-lifetime opportunity, they had agreed. When would they have a spare five thousand dollars again? Never, that's when. And she was the one whose mother had died. It was her money. It was just weird, not knowing exactly where she was or if he'd be able to reach her.

"I want Mommy," Maddie said, as if hearing his thoughts.

"Let's try the pink stuff," he guessed. "Mommy will call later on."

"Ohhhhkaaay," Maddie pushed the covers down and swung her bare feet out of bed, her hair a tangled frame for her pale face. She looked so small in her nightgown, more four than six. Acting on impulse, he swept her up in his arms and gave her a squeeze. She wriggled happily.

"Love you, Froggie."

AGAINST MEDICAL ADVICE

"Love you too, Toad," she giggled, pulling his beard like she always did.

He carried her to the bathroom and set her down, searching through the cupboard until he found the giant bottle of Pepto. He poured her an amount he figured was about right, not bothering to measure, and watched her as she downed it.

She made a face. "Tastes like chalk," she said.

"At least it's pink chalk," he answered, swishing water in the little cup and putting it back in the cupboard. He saw Maddie's chest rising and falling and worried. Why would she be struggling to breathe with a stomach ache? But she smiled up at him, a little of the medicine at the corner of her mouth. He told himself she would be fine and wiped her mouth with a washcloth.

He hated it when his little girl was sick. He had always been terrified something serious would happen to her—leukemia or epilepsy or some other life-altering, life-threatening illness. Ever since she was a baby. It was part of being a parent, Tish always told him, but it felt like more than that. It probably had to do with his mom, although he had trained himself not to think back to her illness that started when he was fifteen, or her death when he was seventeen. Still, sometimes, when Maddie was smaller, he couldn't sleep for the worry.

Tish would always talk him down. She was the calm one between the two of them. It was one of the things that drew him to her; she balanced him, steady and in control. Going off on this cruise was the wildest thing she had ever done. It had thrown him a bit, if he was honest. He had encouraged her to go, but he didn't truly believe she would. Her mom's death had changed her a little. But still, if she were here, she would have taken Maddie's illness right in stride.

"She's fine," he heard her saying. "It's a bug. She's healthy as a little horse. She'll fight it off."

That's all this is, he told himself. *A little bug.*

"Do I have to go to school?" Maddie asked in her sweetest voice.

Frank knew what Tish would say. "Get your little butt ready for school, Madame," she would bark playfully, with a little swat to Maddie's rear.

But his wife was somewhere in Alaska. He gave Maddie a sly smile, which she returned.

"Thank you, Daddy," she grinned. "I looooove you."

He laughed and ruffled her hair.

"Come on, let's get out of the bathroom and get you some breakfast, then I'll call the school."

Maddie didn't eat much of her oatmeal. Maybe she was burnt out on it. He'd given it to her every morning for the past week, he realized. He wasn't the most creative in the kitchen.

"You want some eggs?" he asked.

"No, thank you," she said. "Can I watch some YouTube?"

Frank knew that the videos she would watch would lean toward the spooky. She was always sneakily showing him videos with surprise jump scares.

"How about we put on a movie?"

She made a little face for just a second, but then her face brightened. "*Five Nights at Freddy's?*"

"You're really trying your luck today, aren't you?" he chuckled. "You, little Froggie, are way too young for that movie."

"All of my friends watch it!"

"How about *Soul*?"

She harrumphed.

"What? I love *Soul*!"

"I don't."

"Alright, what else do you want to watch? Nothing scary."

"Fiiiine. Let's watch *Moana*."

"*Moana* it is. Clear your plate."

She dumped her full bowl of oatmeal into the garbage can and snatched a blanket off of her bed, heading to the couch to snuggle in.

....

Maddie was asleep in fifteen minutes, curled beneath her soft blanket. In her sleep, her breathing was definitely labored. Every once in a while, she would whimper a little. Frank touched her fore-

AGAINST MEDICAL ADVICE

head again. Still not hot, but her skin was a little damp. She was sick.

Chapter Two

Shelly's phone was buzzing on her hip, and her heart gave a double-beat, as it always did. As it had for ten years. She had just accepted that every new call would give her that moment of anxiety, which she would push aside to answer, and then she would get to work.

It was her supervisor.

"Hey, Mae, what's up?"

"Welfare check. Neglect."

"How many kids?"

AGAINST MEDICAL ADVICE

"Two. Three and five. Kindergarten teacher called it in. Five-year-old is still in diapers–with a bad rash."

Shelly told herself it was just information. Neglect, abuse, it was her job. The softness that had gotten her into the job had been ground down after the first year. It had to be. She would have quit a long time ago if her heart broke every time she saw a dirty, starved little face in a trash-filled home empty of food. She did hope this one had a working toilet. That level of filth was a little harder to shake. For that she would need her meds. For that, she would have to push away the memories.

"Text me the address, I have time right now."

"Awesome, thanks."

The address came through a moment later and she plugged it into her GPS. It was a neighborhood she knew, not a good one. The white ghetto. At least it wasn't a Black neighborhood. She never felt right pulling the Black kids, as a blond-haired, blue-eyed white lady. Part of her said she didn't have the right. But she'd do it if she had to. And sometimes she had to.

Shelly pulled up in front of the house, knowing that her car looked like that of a social worker or undercover cop. Resisting the urge to pop one of her pills—she was almost out, and it was early, as always—she scoped out the house. There was a "Keep Out" sign in one of the front windows. She heard dogs barking.

She called Mae.

"This may need to be a co-response," she said. On rougher cases the social workers were required to request a police officer escort, ever since that shooting in Mayton.

"Let me see if they have anybody available, hold on."

Shelly waited, hoping it was Rogers and not Sinclair or one of the others.

"They don't have anyone right now; there's apparently a stand-off in Acres. You'll have to wait."

The barking dogs had quieted down. Shelly eyed the house. There was a pot of dead flowers on the porch.

"It's fine, I'm good I think."

"You think?"

AGAINST MEDICAL ADVICE

"Yeah, I'm good."

"Check in in fifteen."

"Will do."

Almost without thinking about it, Shelly washed down a Xan before getting out of her car. She locked her doors behind her, went to the porch, and knocked. The doorbells were always broken, so she had stopped bothering. She heard a scuffling behind the door, but then nothing. The kids were probably home alone.

"Hey, sweetie, are you okay in there?" she said loudly and waited. "I'm here to help you!"

"My mommy's not home," she heard a small voice. A boy, she thought.

"Can you unlock the door? I just want to check and make sure you're alright." She couldn't go in the house without a court order—or unless she believed the child was in immediate danger—but she wanted to lay eyes on the kids so she could at least start her report. She was willing to push her luck a little.

The door handle clicked. She turned it, but there must have been a deadbolt, because it wouldn't open.

"Can you open the other lock, sweetheart?"

"It's too high!"

"Is there a chair?"

She heard feet scampering and then a dragging noise. *Oh, good.* She heard the deadbolt draw and opened the door. The smell of her childhood hit her in the face like an ocean wave, up her nostrils, in her mouth, choking her. She coughed. Two matted little dogs swarmed around her feet, jumping and barking. She could almost see the fleas dropping off of them.

The little boy in front of her was filthy, naked except for a drooping diaper.

"Good job!" she said to him. "Are you okay?"

"I'm thirsty. And my brother won't wake up."

That double-thump played in Shelly's heart.

"I have a bottle of water in my car, I'll get it for you in just a minute. Where's your brother?"

"He's sleeping."

"Can you go try to wake him up again?"

"I tried! I tried!"

"I'd like to see if he's okay."

"I can't wake him up. He's cold."

Oh, no.

She called Mae and asked for permission to enter the house. Her supervisor wanted her to wait for Rogers.

"I don't think I should. I think something's really wrong."

"Okay. Those notes better be *pristine.*"

"Yes, ma'am."

Shelly stepped into the house. There were blankets taped over the windows in lieu of curtains, and the carpet was wet and reeked of dog urine. The boy led her through a hallway strewn with broken toys and dirty clothes. As soon as she entered the bedroom behind him, her hand flew to her mouth.

"Oh, no," she whispered. "No, no."

Chapter Three

"Okay, I can get her there at ten," Frank said. He hung up, wondering how much money was left on the FSA card. It was November, so not much, he knew. He had skipped a long-haul job to stay home with Maddie while his wife went on her cruise, so things were a little tight. But not so tight he couldn't take his sick kid to the doctor.

Maddie was still sleeping when it was time to go. He woke her up.

"My tummy hurts!" she curled in a little ball.

"That's why I'm taking you to the doctor." He picked her up and she laid her head on his shoulder. He took her to the car and helped her buckle herself into her booster seat. Before he took off, he sent a quick text to Tish, although he didn't know when she would get it.

"Taking Mads to the doctor. I'm sure she's fine but she has a stomach ache and she's sleeping too much."

He waited a moment, but didn't get a reply. He tried not to be angry that she was gone. He knew it wasn't her fault Maddie was sick. These things happen.

He had to carry the little girl into the office; she didn't want to walk. She wrapped her arms around his neck, nuzzling her face into his beard.

"Am I going to get a shot?" she asked. She hated shots with a passion. They always had to hold her down for her vaccinations. He always cried.

"I don't know, Froggie," he said, not wanting to lie to her. "We'll have to see what they say. If you do get a shot, I'll get you ice cream afterward."

"Chocolate."

"Yes, chocolate," he smiled.

The wait was long. Frank tried to interest Maddie in the cartoons on the large overhead TV, but she sat slumped in her seat, her chest heaving again. Her eyes were closed and she was working hard to breathe, minute after minute, for at least an hour. Frank kicked himself for not taking her to the emergency room. But the ER copay was $250. Finally, they were called back by a kindly looking older nurse with tightly curled short gray hair.

Maddie's oxygen level was ninety-three. The nurse's brow furrowed.

"That's not good, right?" Frank asked.

"It could be worse. How long has she been sick?"

"Just since this morning."

"Does she have asthma?"

"Not that I know of."

By the time the doctor came in—a youngish Indian woman—Maddie wanted to go home. The doctor had her lay on the table and palpated her abdomen. Maddie drew her legs up and gave a little screamy gasp that tore at Frank's heart.

AGAINST MEDICAL ADVICE

"What do you think it is?" he asked.

"I'm not sure, these symptoms are a little strange. I don't think it's appendicitis. It could be her bowel, or an infection. We're going to need to do bloodwork and get an MRI. Today."

"Do I have to get a shot, Daddy?"

He picked her up and gave her a hug.

"You do, Froggie. I'm sorry."

Maddie started to cry.

The doctor gave the girl a little pat on the shoulder and told Frank that someone would be in shortly to give them directions for the labs.

Chapter Four

THE LITTLE BOY WAS dead. Shelly didn't know how his brother had thought he was sleeping. His eyes were open, glassy, staring without seeing. White vomit dribbled from his mouth and pooled around his head, cool and sticky. A bottle of bleach, lid off, stood nearby. Shelly took a pulse, just to be sure. The child's arm flopped back to the mattress as though he were a doll.

AGAINST MEDICAL ADVICE

"Did he drink this?" she asked the older child, gesturing toward the white bottle. The boy nodded his head.

"We were thirsty. It tasted bad, though."

Shelly sat back on her heels and closed her eyes for a moment. She hadn't seen a dead child since...since her brother. He had been older than this boy, but still younger than Shelly. She had been eight.

The images of her family's kitchen, filthy and spattered with her brother's blood, transposed themselves over the dingy room where this new child lay dead and his brother stood leaking tears, diaper drooping and stinking.

Shelly felt like screaming, screaming like she had when her brother lay limp on the kitchen floor, their mother peering down at him, her eyes wild with the drugs and the rage, the claw hammer still in her hand. Shelly remembered how her brother had twitched on the floor, gasping rhythmically before going rigid and then still.

RUTH ANNA EVANS

She remembered the police, and the ambulance, and that there were no sirens when they took him away.

Two dead children. And for both, Shelly couldn't do a damn thing to help.

Chapter Five

Maddie screamed the whole time they took her blood. It took Frank and two techs to hold her still enough, and even so they had to search for her tiny vein. Tears were running down Frank's face by the time they withdrew the little butterfly needle from his daughter's arm. She squirmed away before they could put the band-aid over the bubble of blood that welled out of her, and it smeared on Frank's shirt. There were red marks on Maddie's arms where the tech had pinned her down. Those marks would bruise, Frank knew.

If Maddie's mom were there, she would gather Maddie in her arms now and hold her until she stopped crying. That was the routine. Dad held her for shots, Mom comforted her after. But Tish didn't even know what was happening.

"How long before we get results?"

"It should be today; your doctor put a rush on them," the young woman answered, her glasses askew from the battle with the child.

"Thank you." He stroked Maddie's hair as she bawled into his shoulder. "We have an MRI to do?"

"Go through those doors and check in at the window."

"Thank you," he said again and carried Maddie down the hall. Her sobs had turned into whimpers.

At least the MRI wouldn't hurt, he told himself.

The wait was long. He could tell Maddie still didn't feel well because she didn't ask to play on his phone; she just sat slumped against him, working harder than she should to breathe. He fought the panic tendriling up into his chest. He had to stay calm. He was doing what he should be doing.

His phone dinged. It was Tish.

"Did you get her to the doctor?"

"We're here now."

"Is she okay???"

"I'm not sure. They took blood."

"I'm so sorry. I wish I were there."

"I wish you were too."

"Keep me posted."

"I will."

"I love you."

"You too, babe."

He paused. He didn't want to worry Tish so much that she couldn't enjoy her trip. Probably Maddie just needed some antibiotics.

"How are the whales?" he tapped out.

"Daddy, is that Mommy?"

"Yes, sweetie, do you want to tell her 'Hi'?" he handed the phone toward his daughter. She pushed it back.

"Tell her to come home."

"*The whales are hiding, lol,*" Tish texted back. Frank didn't have it in him to *lol*. He put his phone away.

"Maddie?" It was their turn.

Frank took Maddie by the hand and guided her back into the imaging lab. She walked this time, which eased his mind a bit. She was clutching his hand.

"Are they going to give me another shot?" she asked.

"No, baby, not this time."

"Um, actually we do have to inject her with some dye for the imaging," the nurse, a middle-aged white woman said softly, looking at Maddie.

"Noooo!" Maddie protested. "Please, no, I just had a shot!" She pulled back on Frank's hand. "NO."

Frank's heart sank. He reached out to pick Maddie up and she kicked at him. She was six, not three, and she was small but not so small that she could be lugged like a sack of potatoes despite her thrashing. Besides which, she had to be still for the MRI. He had to get her calm.

He knelt down on the floor next to her.

"Froggie, I'm so sorry this is happening. We have to do this to get you better."

"I'm better! My stomach doesn't hurt anymore! The pink stuff worked. Please, let's just go home."

"We have to find out why you are feeling so sick and why your breathing is hard. I know you don't want to, but I need you to be good for this." He said it slowly, looking her in the eyes. She looked back at him, her bottom lip trembling.

"I just had a shot."

"I know, sweetie. I'm sorry. Please?"

She gave a little nod and gripped his shoulder, pulling herself to her feet. "Will it hurt?" she asked the nurse.

"It shouldn't," the woman said, then paused. "Sometimes it burns a little, but it will be over fast."

Frank's heart, which was still in his stomach, turned to lead as he saw his daughter go pale.

"It burns?" she whispered.

"Not usually. Usually it's just a prick."

"Do you want me to carry you again?" Frank asked the little girl.

"No. I'll walk." She squared her shoulders and the nurse led the way to a room and handed Frank a hospital gown that was far too big for Maddie.

"Someone will be in shortly to take her back," she said. "You can of course go with her." She glanced at Maddie. "You'll have to take her earrings out."

Frank nodded. He didn't know anything about earrings, but he nodded. He was the dad. He could do this.

He helped Maddie strip to her underpants and tied the gown around her.

"Let's get your earrings out, sweetie."

"Why?"

"I think the machine uses magnets. We don't want your ears to get stuck!" He tried to make it a joke, but Maddie didn't laugh. She put her hands on her ears.

"I want Mommy," she said.

AGAINST MEDICAL ADVICE

"I know, baby," he answered, reaching over and fumbling with the earring back with sausage fingers. "Me too."

"Don't lose them, they're my diamonds," the girl said. Maddie had begged and begged to get her ears pierced. Tisha didn't have a problem with it; Frank had been the holdout. He couldn't stand the image of a needle stabbing through his daughter's tender earlobes. Tisha had finally taken her, calling him on the way to the mall and informing him that's what she was doing. When Maddie came home a little teary eyed and so proud, he knew his wife had made the right call.

Frank looked around for a place to put the earrings. There was a bag for her clothes and belongings, but the little jewels would be swallowed up in there. He just looked at them in the palm of his hand.

"There's a little baggie over there," Maddie said, pointing. There was, and Frank put the earrings in one of the baggies and slipped it into the bigger bag.

The curtain on their little room slid back.

"Are we ready in here?" The tech this time was a strong-looking young man with tattooed arms, and he was pushing a hospital gurney. Frank helped Maddie climb on and walked alongside the gurney as it glided down the hallway.

He remembered this part, the endless hospital hallways, from his mother's illness. They wouldn't ever let him go back into the procedure rooms, but he always followed as long as he could. In the early days, the techs would look at him askance, clearly wondering why someone so young was doing a grown-up's job, but there was no adult. There was only him and his mother. She had him, and he would make it okay. He went to every appointment, slept at the hospital every night he could.

But in the end it wasn't okay. It wasn't okay at all.

This time would be different. This time he wouldn't let anything bad happen.

Quiet tears were running down Maddie's scared little face. He brushed them away as they walked.

"You're alright, sweetie," he said. "I'm here."

Chapter Six

Shelly dialed Mae's number, shaking. The five-year-old, silent, watched her face. She tried not to say anything that would further traumatize him. She hadn't yet told him his brother was dead, not because she wasn't sure—the body was cold—and not because it wasn't her job—it was—but because she couldn't bring herself to do it. Siblings in neglect situations bonded tightly. He was probably his brother's caregiver. He would blame himself. Just like she had.

Mae was soon on her way and so were the paramedics, so when she heard someone stomp into the house, that's who she expected.

It was the mom.

"What the fuck are you doing in my house?"

Shelly was filled with rage, which she pushed down, trying to find some remains of the artificial calm the Xanax should be providing.

She moved aside so the woman could see her child on the bed. The woman blinked. She was a thin woman, about thirty, worn down beyond her years. She wore a slinky tank top and short shorts, but the effect was sad, not sexy, with the tell-tale havoc wreaked by drugs on her face and in her limbs. It was always drugs, Shelly thought. Drugs and mental illness.

The mom pushed past Shelly to the boy on the bed. She gave him a futile shake, then rounded on the other boy.

"What happened? You were in charge!"

The little boy started crying and darted away from his mother, hiding behind Shelly.

"Don't touch him!" Shelly said, her rage cracking through her calm. She thought she might take a swing at the woman if she didn't let up on her traumatized son.

But the woman let her hands fall to her sides and stood looking at the dead child on the bed.

"He drank bleach," Shelly said, stating the obvious. "Was the water off?"

"I was out making money to get it turned back on," the mother said. Shelly wondered from her outfit what she might have been doing to make that money, and whether she would really have used it for the water, but decided both questions were now irrelevant.

At that moment, Shelly's heart held no sympathy for the woman. She just hoped the police would arrive soon and put her in handcuffs so she could try to find her remaining child a safer place to stay.

It was silent in the room but for the sound of the five-year-old crying. The mother sank to the floor and put her head in her hands.

"What's your name?" Shelly asked the little boy. He didn't stop crying to tell her.

"Jeremiah," the mother said softly, without raising her head. "His brother's name is Ezekiel."

Shelly's heart did twinge with sadness for the mother then. Not for the woman in front of her, but for the person who held her sons as infants, naming them with love and care. Jeremiah and Ezekiel were beautiful names for boys. What had happened that she left them alone, filthy and without food or water?

A lost job, the wrong man, an old friend with a habit—whether it was a crisis or a small moment that changed the trajectory of their lives, the people whose children she took usually started out loving and caring for their children. At least the mothers. The fathers gave less of a fuck, usually. Her own father, for example. The asshole was better off absent. For the kids she helped, too, the dads either weren't around or left bruises if they were. The fathers made her angry; the mothers made her sad. Usually.

AGAINST MEDICAL ADVICE

But usually she wasn't faced with a child's corpse, and today she was fuming. She almost asked the woman cruelly whether the drugs were worth it when she heard the blip of a police siren and then the heavy step of an officer.

Please let it be Rogers, she said to herself.

It was. An older man near retirement, he was always a sight for sore eyes with his entirely bald head and kind eyes. He was the one officer she trusted. The others were uniformly unconcerned with protecting children from further trauma and would haul this mom away from her child kicking, biting, and screaming, if that was what it took. Rogers wouldn't let it come to that.

He moved directly to the boy on the bed, feeling for a pulse.

"Fill me in," he said to Shelly, completely ignoring the mother and taking in the sight of Jeremiah, still crying.

"We got a report of neglect. Jeremiah told me his brother wouldn't wake up, so I entered the home and found Ezekiel. His mother arrived soon after."

"Did you try resuscitation?"

"It was too late." *It was, wasn't it?* She felt a spark of panic. *Could I have saved him?* But no, the boy had been cold, without a pulse. Hadn't he? Had he? *Oh, God. I should have tried.*

She heard the ambulance pull up outside and wanted to tell them to turn their siren off, that there was no point in hurrying. But she did want to get Jeremiah out of the room before they loaded his brother onto the gurney and took him away. For some reason it felt better that way.

Saying nothing to the boy, she took him by the hand and led him out the door of the bedroom. He followed her, but he kept his eyes on his little brother until they turned the corner into the hall. Then he crumpled to the ground and wouldn't budge. She leaned over and picked him up, her nose wrinkling at the smell of his soiled diaper.

"Come on, sweetheart, let's get you out of here and cleaned up."

"Is my brother going to wake up?"

"No, Jeremiah. He died."

The boy didn't speak again as she carried him out of the house. She met Mae coming up the step.

"I heard the radio call," her boss said without preamble. "The mother's inside?"

"Probably headed to jail," Shelly said.

Mae nodded. "Good."

"Do we have anywhere open for a five-year-old boy?" Shelly asked, hoping so hard. This little one did not need the group home, not right now. He needed a goddamn mother.

"Yes, the Rosens have room. I just got off the phone with Mary."

"Thank God."

"Yes, thank God."

Chapter Seven

THE DYE INJECTION DID hurt. It burned. By the time it stopped burning, Maddie's voice was raw.

....

The banging of the MRI terrified the little girl. She couldn't hold her breath but dissolved into a fit of coughing, and then wouldn't try again. The technician tried to soothe her and convince her to lay still, but she was thrashing her limbs inside of the machine, banging her head against the restraint and begging her father to get her out.

"Daddeeee! Daddy, please!" The girl was crying so hard she couldn't breathe. Frank felt like he was going to hyperventilate himself.

"Can we pull her out, please, just for a minute? This isn't working." He looked through the screen at the tech, a Latina woman with a stern face.

The red light on the machine clicked on and the tray holding his daughter slid out. Maddie lunged for his neck and clung to him.

He peeled her off.

"I'm better, I'm better, please, can we just go home?"

"We can go home right after we do this. It's just loud noises, it won't hurt you."

"I'm scared."

"I know." He was at a loss. He hugged his daughter and racked his mind for something that would convince her to lie still. He had nothing.

She sniffled.

"I really have to?" she asked.

"Yes, you really have to."

"And it won't hurt? Really and truly?"

"Really and truly. It's just a picture."

"Okay, I'll do it. But we have to go home after. Do you promise?"

"I promise."

"Okay. Give me a kiss," she demanded.

He kissed her on her head and her cheek, awed by her bravery, and laid her back down on the platform. She gave a thumbs up. The machine hummed and drew her back inside it. Frank's heart beat hard. The banging started. He heard Maddie whimper but she didn't cry out. He prayed for it to end.

Finally, the machine was silent and the light switched again to red. She came out with a big smile.

"I did it, Daddy!"

"You did, sweetie, I'm so proud of you."

"And we can go home now?"

"We can." He looked at the tech with a question on his face. She came out of the enclosure.

"Your doctor will be in touch with the results as soon as they are available," she said.

AGAINST MEDICAL ADVICE

"Did I do good?" Maddie asked.

The tech cracked a smile. "You did great, honey."

"Do I get a sucker?"

"Um...We don't have suckers, but I think they have some stickers at the front desk?"

"We'll get you a sticker, baby. You ready to go?"

"Yes, PLEASE." Her chest was heaving. Frank told himself it was a little less than before.

Frank stopped by the front desk and let Maddie pick out a sticker—Ariel—and then took her to the car and snapped her into her booster seat. He knew she could do it herself, but he was feeling particularly protective.

She seemed to be doing a little better. Maybe all of this was for nothing. He hoped it was all for nothing.

The phone rang. It was a number he didn't recognize, but he answered it, thinking it may be Tish. The last time he had texted her he had just said they were going to have some tests done, trying not to alarm her. The line crackled and her voice came through, edged with worry. He could tell she was trying to stay calm.

"Is she okay?"

He paused. "She is," he finally said. "We're going home."

"Do they know what's wrong?"

"They're supposed to call me."

"I'm so sorry I'm not there. I talked to the captain and the next place they can let me off to catch a flight is two days away."

The silence hung on the line. He wanted to agree with her, tell her she should be there, tell her to get her ass home now. But he knew she wanted nothing more than to be there.

"Tell me my baby is okay," she said, tears in her voice.

"She's okay. I got her."

"I love you," Tish said.

"I love you too, honey."

They didn't have anything else to say, but they stayed on the line, Frank sitting in the car without turning the key, listening to his wife try not to cry.

AGAINST MEDICAL ADVICE

....

The doctor called three hours later and Frank snatched up the phone. Maddie's stomach was hurting again. She was in the bathroom trying to throw up.

"We didn't find anything," the woman said. "How is she doing?"

"She's nauseous."

"Does she need to be admitted?"

How was he supposed to make a decision like that? Visions of tubes and wires and his scared daughter in a hospital room jumped to Frank's mind. And so did the beyond-certainty that they could not afford a hospital stay.

"I'm not sure. What do you think?"

He wasn't going to let his own fear or financial concerns keep his daughter from getting better. If she needed to be in the hospital, she needed to be in the hospital.

"How is her breathing?"

RUTH ANNA EVANS

She hadn't been struggling to breathe as much this afternoon, at least, he didn't think so. Now it was mostly the stomachache and nausea.

"I'm going to say keep her home for now unless she gets dramatically worse, but we need to get her in for a colonoscopy and endoscopy."

Frank was horrified.

"A colonoscopy on a *six-year-old*?"

"Yes. I know. I'm sorry."

She told him the procedure center would be giving him a call and to hang tight.

....

They called at 4:35 p.m. and told him they could get her in the day after tomorrow. They gave him prep instructions, which sounded terrible, and said they would email him information about what she could and couldn't eat. Normally, they said, she had to be on a special diet for several days, but the doctor had put a rush on the test.

AGAINST MEDICAL ADVICE

"Oh," the woman said. "One more thing. We ran your insurance and the scopes will cost you $1,200 out of pocket. Up front."

Chapter Eight

MARY MET SHELLY AND Jeremiah at the car with a towel and a stuffed bunny rabbit. She knew the boy was coming with nothing; she was used to that. She helped Shelly get him out of the car and wrapped him in the towel.

"I'm Mary," she said. "You're going to be staying with me for a little bit. I'm going to show you where you're going to sleep, and then we're going to get you cleaned up." She spoke clearly, without smothering the boy or attacking him with information. She was one of the good ones.

Shelly followed Mary and Jeremiah into the house. There were four other children currently placed here, and they were lucky there was an opening. She helped Mary strip the boy and wash him, noting the lice crawling along his hairline. Her scalp itched, and she remembered how difficult it was to find the bugs in her own blond hair the last time they made the jump from a child.

They got out the lice shampoo and scrubbed his scalp with it, then slicked his hair with olive oil and put a rubber cap on him.

The diaper rash was bad. Really bad. Shelly winced to see it. Mary applied the Desitin gently and put him in a pull-up. Potty training would wait.

They had both done this before, too many times.

Some social workers felt that their job stopped at drop-off, but for Shelly it helped her heart to know that the kids had someone who followed them through to when they were clean and dressed and fed before leaving. And it was a two-person job.

Mary sat Jeremiah at the kitchen table with a bowl of noodles. Shelly followed her into the living room.

"His story?"

"He was home alone with his younger brother. No water. The brother drank bleach and…he died." Shelly couldn't help it; her voice broke.

Mary gave her a hug.

"I'm sorry."

"I'm sorry for that little boy. The mother said he was 'in charge.'" You know that means he's going to blame himself."

"I'll get him signed up for services."

"Thank you. Do you need anything else?"

"Does he have any belongings at all? Is anything salvageable?"

"It wasn't meth, so maybe. I'll go back and check."

"Do it tomorrow," Mary said. "You need to go home tonight."

"No, if he has a comfort object, he will need it tonight."

"I'll ask him," Mary said. She popped her head back in the kitchen. "Sweetie, do you have a stuffie? A bear?"

His eyes brightened a little. "My doggie," he said. "I left my doggie."

Shelly nodded. "I'll get it," she said.

Mary gave her another hug. "Thank you," she said.

....

Shelly steeled herself to go back in the house. She popped one, then two, of her pills. She couldn't remember how many she had taken today. She forgave herself; it had been a hard day.

The house was dark with police tape around it. A few officers were still there. They must be gathering evidence for serious charges. *Good.* Again, she was glad it was Rogers. Sinclair in particular would have left it at the easier to prove neglect, not taking the extra effort to back up negligent homicide. That bleach should have been child-proof at the very least. The kids should not have been alone without water. The kids should not have been alone.

Shelly found the stuffed blue dog in the room where Ezekiel had died, on the other of the twin mattresses on the floor. It was dirty, as she expected, and old. One of the ears was coming off.

"Can I take this?" she asked the cop who was taking pictures of the room.

"Um."

"The little boy needs it."

"Okay. Let me take a picture of it."

Shelly couldn't imagine what a picture of a stuffed dog would add to the case, but she put it back on the bed where it had been while he snapped a photograph, then picked it back up. She saw another stuffed dog on the dead brother's bed, matching except red instead of blue. They looked like the kind of stuffed animals you would win at the fair. She hoped the little boys had some happy memories like that tucked away somewhere.

AGAINST MEDICAL ADVICE

She picked up the other stuffed animal and raised her eyebrows at the officer. He shrugged and nodded. She thanked him and headed out.

Mary was grateful for the stuffed animals but didn't invite Shelly in. She was ready to start establishing the child's routine. Part of Shelly wanted to give them to the boy herself, see something other than sorrow on his face, but she understood. Her job, for now, was done.

On the way home, she stopped by the grocery store and picked up a bottle of wine. It was a bottle-of-wine night.

Chapter Nine

THEY HAD FIVE HUNDRED dollars in savings. They had just dropped everything to fix the truck's transmission and were in the process of building their emergency fund back up. They had almost...ALMOST...put that money from Tish's inheritance into the savings account and left it there, but Frank had convinced her to take this one chance to make a lifetime memory. "In the bank it's just money," he remembered saying. "Money isn't what matters." And now money was the only thing that mattered. If they didn't get Maddie the treatment she needed, they would never forgive themselves for throwing those thousands away.

They didn't have a credit card; they'd dug out of that hole a couple of years ago and pledged not to get buried again. He wasn't sure their credit would allow them to get one right now anyway, but he couldn't think of anything else. So he got on the phone and tried.

After working his way through the automated menu and waiting on hold several times, he was approved, for three thousand dollars at an eighteen percent interest rate. It would have to do.

"How soon can I access the funds?"

"Your card will go in the mail today, you can use it as soon as it arrives in five to seven business days. Just call the number on the front to activate it."

"I need to use the funds immediately. Is that possible?" He held his breath.

The representative, a friendly woman named Jean, paused.

"What amount do you need available now?" she asked.

"Twelve hundred."

"Let me check. Can you hold?"

"Yes."

"Daddy?" Maddie came out of her bedroom. She looked pale.

"Yes, baby?"

"Can I have a popsicle? I have a bad taste in my mouth."

He shuffled his phone to his shoulder and reached in the freezer, rooting around for a blue popsicle, her favorite. He could only find red.

"Is red okay?" he asked apologetically. Maddie made a face but then nodded.

"Can you open it for me?"

"Of course."

The woman came back on the phone as he was searching for the scissors.

"We can approve a limit of five hundred dollars immediately," she said.

"Is there any way to bump that up to seven hundred?" he asked, feeling like he was begging. He only had the five in the savings and not much left in the regular checking. They still had to eat.

AGAINST MEDICAL ADVICE

"I'm sorry, the five is the best we can do."

"Okay, thank you."

"I just need your email address and I can send you the temporary credentials," she said.

He gave it to her, thanked her and hung up. The popsicle was starting to melt. He found the scissors in the junk drawer and gave the sweating mess to Maddie.

"Why do we need seven hundred dollars?" she asked, sucking on the ice.

"You don't need to worry about that, Froggie, I'm just taking care of something."

"Is it for the doctor?"

"Yes. You have to have a test."

She stopped eating her popsicle. "What kind of test?" she asked suspiciously. "I just did a test."

"They didn't find anything. They have to do another test." *If I can pay for it,* he thought.

"Will it hurt?"

He didn't know much about colonoscopies and endoscopies, just that you had to prep for them and old people always complained that it was awful.

"I think they make you sleep during the test," he guessed.

"So it doesn't hurt?"

She had been through so much pain in the last day. He didn't know what to say. He didn't want to tell her it wouldn't hurt and be wrong; she'd stop trusting him, and he needed her to trust him.

"I just don't know. It won't hurt bad if it does hurt. And then we can make you better."

His phone buzzed that an email had come through.

He scanned through the diet restrictions: no red dye. "Shit!" he said.

"Daddy! You cussed!"

"I'm sorry. I shouldn't have given you that popsicle; you can't have anything red until your test. Or any nuts, or…" he scanned the list.

"You can have soup!" he said, trying to sound cheerful. "You like soup!"

"I like POPSICLES," she said, her bottom lip sticking out. He gently took the mostly-melted thing from her hand.

AGAINST MEDICAL ADVICE

"I'm sorry." He felt like he had said that a hundred times just today, and had a feeling he would be saying it a thousand more.

Chapter Ten

The next day Shelly woke with a splitting headache and an awful taste in her mouth. Another night where she had that last glass and emptied the bottle. She had dreamed of her old house, the one she left when her brother died. In her dream, she was hiding in the closet, clasping him to her trying to keep him from crying too loudly. Even in her dream, she could feel his little body shaking, feel the wet from his tears and snot soaking through her shirt. Their mom was looking for them with the paddle, drunk and angry. What they were being punished for, Shelly would never know

Shelly's little brother wouldn't remember a time that their mother was nice, but she did. She had a shining memory of her mother braiding her hair for school pictures when she was five. She had smoothed her hair back with gentle hands and smiled at Shelly in the mirror. Shelly had smiled back, and felt so loved.

It wasn't too long after that when Shelly's mom started drinking more. Shelly never knew why it started, just that it never stopped. That it got worse, and then the drugs, and then the hard drugs. And no more smiles in the mirror. No more smiles at all.

Shelly stumbled to the kitchen and found her Xanax on the table. Her hand to her head, she shook the bottle to see how many pills were left. It rattled, almost empty. The stock had shrunk considerably in the past twenty-four hours.

She was going to run out. Soon.

"No more for a couple of days," she said to herself. "No matter what." The doctor tracked how often she requested her prescription, and if she did it early one time too many, they would cut her off completely. So she needed to slow down.

What if there are more dead kids? she challenged herself. *What then?*

For that she would allow herself one. Or two.

It was her day off. Shelly took three Excedrin Migraines, worried about her liver, and went back to bed.

An hour later after staring at dead brothers behind her eyelids for as long as she could stand, she got up and took a pill. Two left.

Half an hour later, the room spun her to sleep.

Chapter Eleven

THE PREP. SUCH A small word for such a thing. At first she refused to drink "the stuff," as they called it.

"It stinks!" she moaned.

Then he convinced her to taste it. She spit it out.

"EW!"

He had nothing to bribe her with because she couldn't eat. Her mother wasn't home to soothe her. Eventually, they were both in tears.

"Okay, okay, I'll do it!" she finally wailed, when he collapsed in a chair, his head in his hands.

He poured her a glass and handed it to her, having no advice on getting it down. She looked at him reproachfully and swallowed.

She drank the whole glass, making gagging noises. Then she immediately threw up everywhere.

He cleaned her up, pulling her soaked shirt over her head, trying not to get the vomit on her face. When she was clean, he picked her up and held her until she fell asleep.

··········

"She couldn't do it. I'm sorry. She tried and she couldn't."

The nurse sighed. "Can she take pills?" Frank knew she was just trying to get her job done, but he wished she was more sympathetic. His daughter was six.

"Sometimes?"

"Like, a lot of pills?"

"I don't know. Maybe."

"We'll call in a prescription. Try again today and we'll fit you in late in the day tomorrow."

⋯⋯⋯⋯

The woman wasn't joking about a lot of pills. There were twenty-four.

Maddie started choking them down. She didn't throw up.

Thirty minutes later she got a look on her face and ran for the bathroom.

Diarrhea, pills, diarrhea, pills.

Maddie pooped and pooped until she was just spurting yellow water. Her little bottom was so sore she wouldn't let him wipe her. He said 'fuck it' and just didn't. Let the doctor deal with it. He needed Tish.

⋯⋯⋯⋯

Maddie was quiet on the drive to the colonoscopy center. But once they got back and she was tucked under the clean white sheets, she perked up. The nurses were kind and gentle, coaxing little smiles onto her tired face.

"Does your stomach still hurt?" he couldn't keep himself from asking. Maybe she just needed a good cleanout. Maybe it was constipation.

Her brow furrowed and she nodded sadly. He decided not to ask again. If she was going to try to ignore her pain, he would let her. But her chest was still working too hard to get a breath in, off and on but still enough to notice. Frank could feel his own panic growing. How would a colonoscopy and endoscopy diagnose a breathing problem? Everything seemed wrong to him. But he wasn't a doctor. He was just a broke guy with a sick kid.

As they wheeled her back—he had asked to go with her but was relieved when they said no—Frank slumped into his chair, relieved that for a little while his daughter was in someone else's hands.

Chapter Twelve

FRANK TRIED TO REST while Maddie was back in the procedure room, but his phone kept buzzing. Tish was panicking. She had arranged to get off the boat at the next stop and then hire someone to drive her to the nearest airport, but she was in a remote stretch of Alaskan waters. The stop was still half a day away, and the drive from that stop to the nearest airport was another day. Then the flight, then the drive home in a rental car. The airlines had agreed to switch her flight due to the emergency—thank God they had bought the insurance—but they weren't sure where the money for the rental car would come from. They were flat broke.

Eventually he stopped answering her texts–she would understand–and just sat, hands folded tightly. He had waited like this so many times with his mother. Being here reminded him of her. Eventually she had started smelling like a hospital, even at home. As though hospital oozed out of her pores. He always thought of it as a green smell, whatever that meant. Chemicals and sickness. And then when she died, at home one night while he was sleeping, that tiny part of him had been relieved he wouldn't have to smell it anymore.

This hospital smelled the same.

A tech wheeled a sleeping Maddie into the bay where Frank waited. He watched her as her eyelids flickered and stroked her hair as she came to.

AGAINST MEDICAL ADVICE

"Where's Mommy?" was the first thing she asked, blinking away the anesthesia. "My tummy hurts. I want Mommy."

Frank felt that irrational flare of anger again, but tamped it down.

"I'm here, Froggie. We'll call your Mommy in just a bit, okay?"

Maddie scowled and rolled over in the hospital bed with its white sheets, now wrinkled. "Tell her to come home," she said, her voice muffled with tears.

"She's coming, baby."

Maddie didn't say anything. Frank stroked her hair again, but she shook him off.

"Do you need anything?"

"I need my Mommy."

....

Later that day, when Maddie was sleeping, the doctor called. The colonoscopy was inconclusive.

"That rules out my biggest worry, an obstruction," she said. "But her white blood cell count was a little elevated in the latest blood work. I'm going to prescribe an antibiotic."

"But why is she having stomach pain? Why is she having trouble breathing?"

"It could be functional bowel pain. Let's see how the azithromycin works and then take it from there."

Frank didn't want to question the doctor, but something didn't sound right to him.

"A z-pack? You're giving her a z-pack? My kid is really sick!"

Dr. Curry hesitated, then said quietly, "Your insurance requires that we take that step when the white blood cell count is high and there's not another explanation. I would run more tests, but they won't approve them without the azithromycin," the doctor admitted.

"How long does she have to be on it before we move on?" Frank couldn't believe what he was hearing.

"Five days. Unless she gets substantially worse."

AGAINST MEDICAL ADVICE

Frank ended the call and looked at his phone. He had refrained from turning to Google, but he couldn't help himself.

Stomach pain heavy breathing white blood cell count elevated, he typed in.

The list of possible ailments took his breath away. Leukemia. Peritonitis. Gastrointestinal bleeding. Frank's head swam and he remembered that feeling that had overcome him when he held his baby daughter for the first time. That feeling that he was going to fuck it all up, that he wasn't up to the responsibility, that someone else had better be in charge. That feeling had passed over the years of routines and safety, but now all safety was gone. And they had given him a z-pack. A whole lot of expensive, painful tests and now nothing.

He had to do something. Now.

Chapter Thirteen

Shelly was out of pills. She hadn't been able to slow down as she had promised herself she would, and now she was in her car preparing to do a welfare check staring at the bottom of an empty bottle.

Her hand was shaking. It was too soon for full-blown withdrawal, but not too soon for her everyday anxiety to grasp her heart with cold fingers and give it a squeeze.

She snapped the lid back on the bottle and took a deep breath.

"You are not an addict," she said out loud. "You just went a little too fast through your prescription. It's been a stressful week." That was an understatement. But for a not-addict, she had spent a lot of time since the boy's death bombed out of her mind.

Her mom's addiction hadn't been pills, which Shelly thought may explain her own drug of choice. She could convince herself she wasn't like her mother, who had been an alcoholic, like everyone else, but by the end also an intravenous drug user and meth addict filled with rage. Shelly would try to hide, try to keep her little brother safe, but her mom would find them. Until she found them with a hammer in her hand, and Benjamin died in a pool of blood and brain matter.

A year later and three foster homes in, Shelly was informed of her mother's death and given an allowance to buy something for the funeral.

RUTH ANNA EVANS

She pocketed the money and went in her hoodie, only because they made her. She didn't look at her mom's face in the coffin, didn't cry. Why would she cry for the woman who killed her brother? But alone that night, she did cry. She soaked her pillow with tears. She had held onto the hope that her mother would get clean, would come for her, would thank her for trying to save her little brother, would apologize, and mean it. All of that hope was now gone. And Shelly was alone.

These were the thoughts she had when her pill bottle ran empty.

She steeled herself for whatever she was going to find in the next house on her list, and the one after that, and after that. She stilled her shaking hands and went to work.

Chapter Fourteen

Frank was panicking—full-blown panicking. The entire time Maddie was sleeping, he was researching, scrolling desperately on his phone through lists of symptoms and treatments, making a list. It was driving him crazy that no one had been focusing on his daughter's breathing issues. After an hour of listening to her cough and wheeze through her bedroom door, he was convinced she had lung cancer that had gone undetected by the MRI. Or she had asthma that was being ignored, and that an attack at any moment would steal her from him. Or she had contracted some sort of parasite that was eating its way through her insides.

By the time Maddie woke, sleepy-eyed and still worn out, Frank was frantic. He tried not to show it as he tucked the child into a pile of blankets on the couch and put on Little Rascals. She didn't even ask to watch something scary, just stared at the TV, her chest heaving. He realized she hadn't really spoken since the hospital.

"You're going to be okay, Maddie," he told her. She looked at him, dubious.

"Do I have to take more tests?" she whispered. "I don't want any more tests."

"Not today, honey."

She studied his face, as though reading the fear etched there.

"Do you want anything to eat?" he asked her, trying to distract her from his worry.

"Popsicle," she answered, turning away from him.

AGAINST MEDICAL ADVICE

"Of course."

Frank got her a popsicle–all they had left was green–and went back to his list, scrolling down the list of treatments his insurance wouldn't cover. She needed a breathing treatment, he decided. He didn't know why it hadn't been offered in the hospital.

How was he supposed to provide what his daughter needed when his insurance company insisted that she take useless medication for five whole days? She could be dead in five days. Tish could come home to a dead child. She would never forgive him. He would never forgive himself.

I have to do something. I have to do something. I have to do something. The thought wouldn't leave his head as he stood in the living room doorway and watched his daughter struggle to breathe. Her eyes were dull. He could tell she was in pain.

Fuck it. Fuck the doctors. Fuck the tests. Fuck the insurance company. He was her father. It was his job to make her better.

Going to the bathroom, he rummaged around in the cupboard. The Internet said that breathing treatments contained corticosteroids. He remembered some that he had left over from a bad case of poison ivy. It had cleared up quickly once he started the medicine and he had neglected to finish it—didn't like the side effects.

He was a handy guy. He could do this.

He found the blister pack and popped half of the pills out into his hand, the *have to do something* voice drowning out the *bad fucking idea* voice in his head.

He put the pills in a Ziploc bag and, for lack of a better tool, began smashing them with a hammer. Once they were dust, he went back to the Internet.

What can I mix pills with so I can turn them to vapor? he searched, scrolling through the results until he found something that made sense. He needed propylene glycol.

What household items contain propylene glycol?

Bingo. Coca-Cola.

Don't. This is madness. The voice in his head now was Tisha's. But Tish wasn't home, and he was.

Chapter Fifteen

THE NEXT HOUSE WAS dirty but it wasn't filthy. The living room carpet, where Shelly stood awkwardly, was covered in a thin sheen of pet hair. The house smelled of cats, but Shelly's probably did too.

The three brown-eyed, black-haired kids were seated together on the couch, staring at Shelly with pale faces full of fear. This was a case of a bruised arm, spotted by a vigilant teacher. It was a first report. There might not be anything she could do, but she was going to do what she could.

"Which of you is Tonia?" she asked.

The mother, a large, mean-looking woman who was clearly a few minutes from spitting on Shelly, flicked her hand at one of the children, who looked like she wanted to disappear.

Shelly asked the twelve-year-old to join her on the front porch, where she sat down on the step and patted the cement next to her. Wary, the girl sat. Shelly could feel the mother hovering behind the closed front door.

"Can I see your arm, sweetie?"

Tonia held out a thin arm. The purple marks were clearly from fingers.

"Do you mind if I take a picture?"

The girl shook her head. Shelly slipped her work phone out of her bag and snapped a few photos as quickly as she could. They would take more pictures at the doctor's office if Shelly recommended a full work-up. She wouldn't be able to justify a case without something from the child, though.

AGAINST MEDICAL ADVICE

"How did you get these bruises?" she asked.

Tonia didn't answer. Shelly had done a hundred of these interviews—more—but she always kept in mind that for the child, it was often a first. For some children, it was a chance they had been waiting for. For others, there was a reasonable explanation, or it was a one-time mistake, and Shelly could leave with a clear heart. Sometimes, though, this interview was a turning point that made things much, much worse.

Shelly was always determined to avoid the last possibility, even if it meant that things stayed the same. Even if things at home weren't perfect. She knew what the system was like. Kids bouncing from foster home to foster home, facility to facility, split from their siblings. Then aging out, dumped into the world with some paperwork and a few check-ins. No, taking kids away was never ideal. Jeremiah got lucky with Mary, and his removal was a must. But his future, too, was nothing but uncertain.

So as mean as this mom was, she may be the best these children could do.

A lot depended on what the child said now. Shelly would follow her lead.

"It's okay," Shelly said. "You can tell me. It's best to be honest."

"I was wrestling with my sister," the girl said finally, with a little nod like she had made a decision. "She hurt my arm, but she didn't mean to."

Shelly couldn't be sure if the girl was covering for her mom or if she was telling the truth. The bruises looked like an adult hand, and a hard squeeze, not the pinch of another child. But how far did she want to push if the child didn't want her to?

"Do you have any other bruises?"

A shadow crossed the girl's face and she folded her arms across her chest, and Shelly knew she was hiding more.

"No."

"Do you feel safe at home?"

"Yes."

Most of the time, the kids discussed among themselves ahead of time what they would say to the social workers. Most of the time, the kids had

AGAINST MEDICAL ADVICE

a plan. This time, the siblings' plan was to keep quiet.

Shelly's brain was crying out for her Xanax. Her stomach was in knots. She tried to ignore it—focus on the task at hand—but the urgency was building. She found herself, instead of thinking about Tonia and her brother and sister, thinking about where she could get a prescription for a new set of pills. Her doctor had been very clear last time. No new script. He had given her what she was going to get, and if she asked again, he might pull that. She had one option, but she couldn't let herself use it.

Shelly forced her mind back to the child in front of her.

She decided to ask straight out. "Sweetie, does your mom hurt you?"

"No. I told you, my sister grabbed too hard when we were wrestling. Don't take us away. Please."

Okay, thought Shelly. *We don't have room for them anyway.*

She gave the girl her card. "Call me if you need anything," she said. "I want to help."

Tonia's lip trembled a little, but she bit it back.

"Thank you," she said. "But we don't need help."

That's what Shelly had told the one teacher who asked if she was okay, about a month before Benjamin's death. She hoped this little girl wouldn't regret the choice like she had.

Chapter Sixteen

Frank combined the Coke and some water and the powdered steroid in a tiny saucepan. He set it on low and let it simmer, then smiled when a steam rose up.

"Sweetie, can you come in the kitchen?"

"I'm tired, my chest hurts."

"I have something to help with that." Frank went to the couch and lifted Maddie to her feet.

She seemed lighter than she had a couple of days ago, but maybe it was in his head.

He set a step-stool in front of the stove and found a thick towel. He leaned Maddie's head over the pan, not too close, and draped the towel over her head.

"Breathe deep, Froggie, this will help your lungs." He hoped it would, anyway. The doctors weren't doing anything. What choice did he have?

"It stinks!" Maddie said from under the towel.

"I know, I'm sorry. Just breathe it a little bit for me and then we'll be all done."

Maddie complied. He could hear her huffing away under the blanket. His chest squeezed with each breath. Somehow, this had to help.

"Daddy?" Maddie's voice was quiet, muffled, wavering.

He pulled the towel off, alarmed.

"My heart is thumping too much," she said. Her face was pale. Then she collapsed in his arms.

··········

AGAINST MEDICAL ADVICE

The paramedics used smelling salts to wake Maddie to consciousness. Frank stood back, appalled and alarmed. What had he done? He felt like he had been in a state of panic before, but now he knew what real panic felt like. His legs were shaking as his daughter blinked herself awake.

"Do you have any idea what caused her to pass out?" the female paramedic, a young tan-skinned woman with "Shawnacie" on her nametag, asked.

"She–she hasn't been feeling well. She's on antibiotics, but we don't know what's wrong."

Shawnacie nodded. "Do you want us to transport her?"

Dollar signs flew through Frank's head. He didn't know his insurance company's policy on ambulance rides, but they couldn't be anything approaching affordable. And, more importantly, perhaps, it would terrify Maddie.

"No, she seems to be okay now. I'll call her doctor."

"Do I have to breathe that stuff again?" Maddie whispered.

"What stuff, baby girl?" Shawnacie asked.

"She must mean the smelling salts," Frank said quickly. Maddie looked at him, confused.

"No, the stuff on the stove."

Frank had dumped the contents of the pan at some point before the paramedics arrived.

"Oh, I had her breathing some steam for her lungs," he said. "It's something we've always done."

Shawnacie let her gaze linger on his face, as though she knew something wasn't right.

"Are you sure you don't want us to take her in and get checked out?"

He didn't know what Maddie would say, whether she would tell someone about his...experiment. Or what could happen if she did.

"No, like I said, we'll call her doctor and get her in for an appointment."

The paramedics' radios buzzed with traffic.

Shawnacie nodded, and her partner started packing up.

After they left, Frank sat on the couch with Maddie and stroked her hair while she watched TV.

AGAINST MEDICAL ADVICE

The thing was, her breathing was better. A lot better.

Chapter Seventeen

SHAKING IN A CHAIR at the kitchen table, Shelly stared at the black screen of her phone. She knew she shouldn't do it. But she was starting to go into full withdrawal. She couldn't think straight. Her head was buzzing, her hands were trembling so badly she almost couldn't hold her phone. She felt like she might blow up or pass out. Soon, she'd have to miss work, and when she missed work, all she could think about was that some kid wouldn't get helped. That it would be the kid who had been waiting years for someone to ask the question, and that by the time she got to him, it would be too late. Another dead child stacked on her conscience like driftwood after a storm.

Her mind was spinning. She felt detached from her body. She watched as her fingers swiped at the screen and found the number. She'd only called it once before, and had hung up before Barbie answered. The arrangement she made with Barbie may have been the worst thing Shelly had ever done, besides letting her little brother die.

She hit the contact, and waited, the best part of her praying the woman wouldn't answer. But she did.

"Hi, Shelly," the woman said, in a voice too deep for her name. "Trying to take my kids away again?"

"Do I need to take your kids away again?"

"No. I'm clean. Or clean enough."

The worst part of Shelly tensed, knowing if this woman really was clean, she probably wouldn't be able to help her.

"What do you need?" Barbie asked.

"I ran out of my prescription early," Shelly said. "I need a script."

"Drug of choice? Still benzos?"

It wasn't a drug; it was medication. She was just short because of the stress. Shelly clung to that.

"Can you do it?"

"Three hundred."

Shelly had the feeling that Barbie was pulling an outrageous number out of the air, knowing Shelly didn't know any better, and knowing that she had no other options for getting drugs illegally.

"Can you do it today?" She gripped her phone, trying not to notice that she was sweating.

"I'll find out." Barbie's voice softened. She knew the feeling.

"Thank you."

"You're welcome. PayPal me the money."

"Up front?"

The soft tone shifted away. "Is that a problem?"

"No. What's your PayPal?"

"I'll text it to you." The woman hung up.

AGAINST MEDICAL ADVICE

A couple of seconds later, Shelly's phone chirped. She transferred three hundred dollars to her checking account out of her dwindling "oh-shit" fund and sent it via PayPal to Barbie, "friends and family." Barbie, she thought to herself, was neither friend nor family. But she was the only one who could help her right now.

She kicked herself for not asking about the kids. When she got the pills, she would. They would be eight and twelve now...no, thirteen. They had been covered in cigarette burns from a shitty boyfriend when Shelly pulled them. Barbie begged, swore she had gotten rid of the man and cleaned up. She also saw Shelly pop a pill at a supervised visit once too many times, and let her know she was on to her.

"If you ever need a refill," she had said. "You can call me. Just give me my kids back."

Shelly told the woman no. Hell no. But when the judge asked if it was in the best interests of the children to return to their mother, she told him yes.

Chapter Eighteen

"Medical records, how can I help you?"

"I'd like to get copies of my daughter's MRI emailed to me, would that be possible?"

"Yes, as long as your doctor has had a chance to review them."

"She said there was nothing on them."

The representative paused, as though reading something in his tone.

"Is there another doctor's office you want them sent to?"

"No, you can just send them to me. Thank you."

"Email?"

He gave it to her, she promised to send it, and he hung up.

If the doctors won't help me, I'll just have to figure this out myself, he thought, pulling up his new medical reference app and resuming his reading on lung conditions.

Maddie was sleeping again. It concerned Frank how much she was sleeping. But her breathing had definitely been better after the incident with the breathing treatment and the paramedics. He was relieved she hadn't said more to them. The female medic had been looking at him strangely. He didn't need anyone poking their nose in.

They can't get you medical treatment, but they can sure take your kids away.

The thought stopped Frank cold. If the state found out he was treating Maddie himself, they really might take her away. He'd obviously never do anything that could really hurt her, but a social worker might not see it that way if she said the wrong thing.

Maybe he wouldn't have to take her back to the doctor. Maybe his plan would work. Maybe everything was going to be just fine.

Chapter Nineteen

Barbie was late. Not a lot late but late enough that Shelly was desperately trying to stave off her third panic attack of the day. *It's going to be okay,* she told herself. She'd have what she needed soon and then she would be fine. It would be plenty to get her to her next refill. And then she'd just be a lot more careful.

A white beater pulled up next to her and Barbie got out. Shelly let out a long breath and got out of her car. Barbie was holding a plastic grocery bag. She handed it to Shelly without a word.

"Thank you," Shelly said.

"You're welcome."

"How are the kids?"

A guarded look sprang to Barbie's eyes.

"They're fine."

"Good." They stood awkwardly for a moment. "Thank you again."

"See you next time." Barbie got back in her still-running vehicle and pulled out of the parking lot.

No next time, Shelly. Promise. Shelly's promises to herself didn't feel like real promises anymore. They felt more like desperate wishes that probably wouldn't come true.

Her phone buzzed.

"Shit!" She didn't answer it, but got back in her car and washed down two Xanaxes with her warm bottle of water.

Then she called Mae back.

AGAINST MEDICAL ADVICE

"Hey, sorry," she said, keeping her voice steady.

"I'm texting you an address, are you free?"

Her heart thumped like it always did, only faster and heavier because the drugs hadn't kicked in yet.

"I am. What's the situation?"

"An EMT did a report after a call. Super vague, I almost screened it out, but if she's right it could turn into something worse so we might as well follow up."

"Injury?"

"No. She said she got a weird feeling that a dad was making his kid sick. He wouldn't let the girl talk to them much, and she said something about breathing something weird. They declined a transport to the hospital."

"Yeah, a little thin, but worth checking into." Shelly started her car, the calm from the pills starting to whoosh back into her brain.

"Let me know what you find out."

"Will do."

Hopefully she wouldn't find anything. But even through the numbness her medication offered, she had a bad feeling about this one.

Chapter Twenty

It was right there on the MRI. Frank didn't know how the doctor had missed it. A lump of something in Maddie's left lung. He compared it to the pictures from the Internet and confirmed that it looked just like the images of lung cancer.

I was right, he thought, with no feeling of vindication. All he felt was frustration and despair. What was he going to tell Tish?

AGAINST MEDICAL ADVICE

He had called the doctor, or tried to. He got blocked by the nurse, who told him not to try to read an MRI himself, and invited him to get a second opinion. But he didn't have time for a second opinion. How long would it take to get in to see a specialist without a referral? His daughter was sick now. While they were sticking tubes into both ends, cancer had been growing in her lung.

The phone rang.

"I'm on my way to the airport, but babe, I don't have any money for the rental car or gas."

"What are we going to do?"

"I already asked Rita. She's short on her rent as it is."

"I got a credit card, but it won't be here for a few days."

"Can we do a cash advance loan?"

They were really scrambling. They'd only done a payday loan once before, early in their marriage when they ran out of toilet paper with two days to go before their paycheck. The bottom really had fallen out, Frank realized. There was no money left.

"I'll see if I can get a pay stub and go over there today," he said. "I'll have to take Maddie with me; there's no one to stay with her," he said, then winced, knowing Tisha felt awful as it was. No need to rub it in.

"I'm so sorry. We should have saved this money; I never should have left," Tisha started beating herself up.

"There was no way to know."

"What do you think is wrong with her?"

He didn't share his suspicion of lung cancer. "Hopefully nothing that this antibiotic won't fix. I'm sure everything's going to be fine."

"I love you, hon. Thank you."

"Love you too."

Frank wanted Tisha to come home to a well child, for them to laugh about how worried they had been. But he heard Maddie's breath rasping through her bedroom door. The reprieve after the breathing treatment had been short-lived.

Frank pulled back up the YouTube video he had been watching. It was a livecast of a surgery. The removal of a lung tumor, one like that he

AGAINST MEDICAL ADVICE

had determined Maddie had. This was the surgery Maddie needed, and no one was doing a goddamn thing to get it for her, himself included.

The camera showed the tray full of instruments, glinting in the bright overhead light. Frank's eyes flicked up and landed on the kitchen knife block.

Chapter Twenty-One

Shelly pulled up in front of the modest but neat little house at the address Mae had sent her. She hoped this was a quick stop; her head was throbbing after the stress of the day. But she needed to make sure the child was okay. EMTs saw all sorts of shit, so if one had been disturbed enough to call something in, she wasn't going to blow it off.

AGAINST MEDICAL ADVICE

She knocked on the door. Very soon, a startled-looking man with a full beard answered. Worry lines were etched into his face.

"Can I help you?" he asked.

"I'm Shelly Daugherty from the Department of Child Services. We received a report from someone concerned about the welfare of your child," she said, as she always did in her neutral tone.

His jaw dropped. He looked shocked, then angry.

"The welfare of my child? My child is sick; all I have been doing is fighting for her 'welfare' and I can't get any help, and now someone has reported me for, what, *child abuse?*"

"Have you taken her to the doctor?"

"Not the right doctor, apparently," he answered, bitter. His eyebrows drew together and for a moment he looked dangerous. Shelly's stomach did a little flip, but in context, she would be angry too.

"What is wrong with her?"

"She is having trouble breathing."

"Has this ever happened before?"

"No. She's always been healthy. You aren't going to try to take her away, are you?"

"Have you been making her sick?" Shelly didn't see any reason to beat around the bush. His reaction to the question—straight out like that—would tell her a lot.

He sighed. "So that's what it is. No. I wish I had been, because then I could stop and she would be better."

Tears filled the man's eyes as he stood in his doorway. He seemed to be clutching the door frame to stay upright. Shelly didn't feel anything for him but sympathy.

"Can I talk to…" she checked her phone for the detail, her memory slippery, "…Maddie?"

"She's sleeping."

"Still, I would feel better if I could talk to her."

"You want me to wake my very-sick child so you can ask her if I made her sick?"

"Yes."

He slumped, then opened the door wider so she could come in. "Fine."

AGAINST MEDICAL ADVICE

Maddie was groggy in her pink Disney princess pajamas.

"Sweetie, I'm Shelly, how are you feeling?"

"I don't want to do any more tests," the little girl said, shaking her dark head.

"You don't have to do any tests for me," Shelly soothed her. "I just needed to ask you a question."

"Okay."

Shelly looked at Frank, who was hovering in the doorway. She stared at him and he stared back at her, but she had more practice and he broke eye contact and faded into the next room.

"Has your Daddy ever hurt you? Ever made you sick on purpose?"

"He held me down for that shot!" Maddie said, her bottom lip puffing out. "And he made me drink that stuff, but the doctor said he had to, that wasn't his fault."

"What stuff?"

"The stuff that was supposed to make me poop, but I couldn't drink it."

"Anything else?"

"No. My daddy is a nice daddy. He doesn't hurt me."

The girl was struggling to catch her breath, and the worry lines on her father's face made sense to Shelly. This was a sick child. Her brown hair was matted around her face, and her lips were as pale as the rest of her face, except for the bruise-like marks beneath her eyes.

Frank walked back in the room, and Maddie went to him and raised her arms to be picked up like a much younger child. Shelly's heart pinched. He swooped the little girl up in big arms and tickled her with his beard, a tired smile playing on his face.

Why am I even here? Shelly asked herself, feeling like an invader.

"I'll let myself out. I'm sorry for bothering you," she said, then made her way to the front door. Frank trailed her without saying anything, as though searching for the etiquette in such a situation.

"I hope she feels better soon," Shelly said over Maddie's head.

AGAINST MEDICAL ADVICE

"Me too."

Chapter Twenty-Two

Since Maddie was up anyway, Frank decided it was a good time to go try to get the payday loan to get Tisha home from the airport once she finally landed.

He felt like a beggar, hat in hand, walking into the run-down box of a building, his pay stub clutched in his hand. He wanted to leave Maddie in the car so she wouldn't see him so humble, but that worry in him imagined her being spirited away by a child rapist, so he brought her in. She took a seat, still in her pink pajamas, on the chipped orange plastic chair along the almost-grimy wall.

The clerk was a heavyset woman with a permanent crease down the middle of her forehead.

"How can I help you?" she said in a surprisingly friendly voice.

"I need to get a loan," he mumbled, scratching his beard the way he did when he was nervous.

"Is this your first time with us?" she asked.

"Yes, ma'am."

She handed him a clipboard with a form to fill out, and he took it back to the tiny chairs and sat next to Maddie, trying to ignore her labored breathing. He wanted to call the doctor's office again, demand a breathing treatment, but he knew they would say no. And if they said yes, he knew that it would be out-of-pocket and his pockets were empty. His mind flashed to the breathing treatment he had concocted, but he couldn't risk her passing out again.

Tish would know what to do. He just needed to get her home.

The max amount allowed for a first-time loan was five hundred dollars. He circled that number then moved on down the form. One of the questions was "When do you anticipate your next paycheck?"

Frank didn't know when his next paycheck was coming; he had to get back on the road to get paid, and he didn't know how he would get back on the road with Maddie so sick. Maybe he could do one-day jobs once Tish was home; but she had to work too. He lied on the form and said he would be paid in two weeks. The hole he was digging was just getting deeper.

"Daddy, I'm tired. Can we go home?"

"Soon, Froggie," he said, then took the form to the desk, along with his pay stub. The woman checked over the form and asked for his ID.

"Do you have your banking account information?"

Dammit. Tisha was the one who handled the checkbook; he knew where one was in the house but hadn't thought to bring it. Now he'd have to drag Maddie all the way back home and then back over here.

"We can issue a check, if that would work better. You'd just have to go to a bank to cash it. We don't give out cash."

"A check would be fine, thank you," he said, relieved. He could go through the drive through at the bank and deposit it into their account. They would do that with just his ID, he thought.

The woman gave him the check for five hundred, and he thanked her. As he walked Maddie out, he spent some brain power on how they would pay the loan back, but the panic that threatened to unleash was too much, and he put the problem away for the moment.

"Can we get ice cream, Daddy?"

"You want ice cream?" he asked, surprised. She'd had no appetite for days, not since the disaster with the colonoscopy prep.

"Yes, please?"

He could spend a little out of the cash advance on ice cream, once he put it in the bank.

He pulled into the bank drive through and waited his turn. But when he sent the check through the tube, there was a longer wait than there should have been. He had a horrible thought, and scrambled his phone out and pulled up the banking app.

Oh no. He was three hundred dollars overdrawn. Fees had stacked up. He hadn't been watching the checking account. Tish had made some purchases, and he had paid the copays at the doctor's offices. But how, how, had he forgotten that he had wiped out the account with the colonoscopy prepay?

Then, the slip came back through. He looked at it. His new balance was $198. He tried not to cry in front of Maddie. Three hundred dollars, just gone. He could get Tish the rental car, maybe, but what about gas? And what were they supposed to use for groceries?

"Can we get ice cream now?" Maddie asked.

He didn't answer.

"Daddeeee, you said ice cream. Please?"

"Yes," he said thickly. "Ice cream."

AGAINST MEDICAL ADVICE

At Dairy Queen he watched her break through the chocolate shell and suck in the ice cream, painting her lips and tongue white.

"Where's yours?" she asked.

"Ice cream makes my teeth hurt," he said, thinking quickly.

"That's sad!"

Tears sprang to Frank's eyes, so he turned his head away and started the truck, driving home in silence except for that incessant whistle of Maddies breath as she slurped her treat.

Pulling up in the driveway, that mad idea that had been tickling his consciousness forced its way to the top.

I could do the surgery on her, he thought. *I could watch the videos and do it. Get the tumor out.*

Immediately, he pushed the thought away, his body cold with the prospect. But now that he had thought it once, he couldn't think about anything else.

Chapter Twenty-Three

Shelly had fucked up. She had fucked up bad. Her hands shook in her lap as she bowed her head and listened to the heavy silence in the room. Mae had said everything there was to say. The girl, the one with bruises, was in the hospital with a broken arm. The girl who had demanded to stay with her mom. The girl Shelly had known was lying.

Mae slid the form across the desk to her.

AGAINST MEDICAL ADVICE

"Fill this out by the end of the day," she said, in a tone that Shelly couldn't read. Her supervisor had always been fair, but this was big. This was the thing they all dreaded, the thing she was supposed to prevent. That it was Shelly's job to prevent. She became a social worker to keep what happened to her as a child from happening to other children. And she had failed.

She felt the urge to reach in her purse and take a pill, but resisted.

Shelly knew, but Mae didn't, that she had been in withdrawal on that home visit. She had not been focused.

"I'm sorry," Shelly said.

"I'm sorry, too," Mae said. "We'll review your notes and there will be a team meeting to determine next steps, if any."

"Next steps?"

"There's a possibility of suspension or a role change," Mae said it matter-of-factly, as she did everything else. "If it's found that you were negligent."

"Oh."

Mae's face softened. "Most likely we're talking about some retraining."

"Okay."

As tough as it would be to be told that the girls' injuries were her fault–Shelly felt that way anyway–the idea of a role change made her catch a hopeful breath. This burden was too great; these kids needed too much. She was not equipped. She was damaged. And she was an addict.

"Should I check on the girl? Move things along?"

"We'll have Dana take over from here. Get the form filled out and work on something else."

Shelly went back to her desk and leafed through files. She wasn't ready to fill out the debrief form; she was afraid that on "contributing factors," she would write down "running out of Xanax." That would be bad. True, but bad.

She came across the file for the little sick girl, the one with the worried father. Why hadn't she closed that case?

AGAINST MEDICAL ADVICE

Starting the process, a little tickle in her brain gave her pause. What if she had missed something there, too?

Chapter Twenty-Four

The texts from Tish were piling up, and Frank didn't know what to do. She was stranded. She had driven out the first tank of gas, and didn't have money for another. She was sitting in the rental car at a gas station, texting him in a panic.

He was just holding his phone, looking at it, swiping back and forth between the messages and the checking account. Everything was red. The credit card hadn't arrived yet. He'd already called all of the friends and relatives who might have money, but none of them did. Tisha didn't have any family left, but she had texted her friends and had come up empty-handed.

"Hang tight, sweetie," he texted, trying to stamp down his own panic. *"We'll think of something."*

"I need to get to my baby."

"I know. I've got her."

"I'm going to call my boss. She hates me, but she has money."

"Okay, hon. Let me know."

He didn't tell her that Maddie was crying quietly in her bedroom, saying her chest hurt. He didn't tell her about the array of items he had on the kitchen table.

Benadryl, three bottles of it.

His sharpest knife, sharpened still further.

Boiled towels.

A plastic sheet.

A needle and some dental floss.

He had the computer on the counter, the MRI image pulled up. The tumor was in her left lung, between her sixth and seventh ribs. He had watched the videos of the surgery he was about to do all night long. He had read medical textbooks, their tiny print peering at him on his phone. His eyes felt heavy and his brain was on fire. Tish's voice had faded to a tiny scream in the back of his head, easy to ignore. If he was observing himself from the outside, he would know that he was losing his grip. He would take himself by the shoulders and order himself to stop. STOP. But he was not on the outside. He was just a dad whose daughter was sick, and no one would help him.

He put his mind to the last problem he had yet to solve. He didn't know how he was going to keep Maddie breathing while he removed the tumor. In a hospital she would be intubated, but he didn't have anything for that here. He had been thinking about the problem all night and had yet to come up with something.

But he was only going to be cutting into one of her lungs, right? She'd still have the other? You could breathe with just one lung…

His phone dinged.

AGAINST MEDICAL ADVICE

"OMG my boss just sent me a hundred bucks, babe! I'm on my way!"

He would have to hurry.

....

Maddie's eyes were drooping, but he still encouraged her to drink more, more of the Benadryl. He tipped the bottom of the bottle up, making sure she drank down to the last drop. He had to get her one hundred percent unconscious.

"Daddy, I don't think I'm 'sposed to..." and then she was snoring against him.

"I love you, Froggie," he said, kissing the top of her head as she slumped in his arms. He lifted her like a baby, clutching her to his chest. He was going to make her better. She was going to be okay. Then he laid her on the plastic-covered table and got the knife.

Chapter Twenty-Five

Shelly tried to leave another message on Frank Weber's cell, but she had filled up the voicemail. She didn't have a number for the mom—the initial report had been very minimal, just the concern of the EMT and that was all.

Probably Frank and Maddie were at the doctor's office and just couldn't answer. Probably she was

AGAINST MEDICAL ADVICE

bothering a perfectly good dad in the middle of a crisis.

Shelly's hands were shaking again. She reached for her purse, for a Xanax, but then thought of the little girl with the broken arm. She had been more worried about drugs than a child.

Mae walked by her desk.

"Get me that form by the end of the day," she said.

"Will do; I just need to check on something first," Shelly answered.

Mae gave her a look.

Shelly threw her purse over her shoulder, the bottle of pills rattling loudly, and headed for the door.

Chapter Twenty-Six

Frank ignored the ringing of his phone. His wife was on her way home, and he needed to have this done by then. She would stop him, but once it was done, there was nothing she could do. She would see the tumor and admit he did the right thing. The doctors wouldn't even admit the tumor existed, but he could see it on the scan, plain as day.

AGAINST MEDICAL ADVICE

"God help me," he prayed aloud, then began to slice between his daughter's ribs. At first, the flesh parted easily and the blood wasn't more than the towel could absorb. She gasped in her sleep but didn't wake. He was glad he had tied her hands and feet down.

As he had seen on the videos, he started to cut through the layer of muscle, but his knife wasn't sharp enough. Swearing, he glanced around the kitchen and his eyes landed on the knife block. The serrated bread knife might get through the muscle. He darted over and snagged it. With some awkwardness and sawing, he got through, trying not to see how torn the muscle was left. He found himself faced with a pinkish-gray barrier. Her lung. It was moving rhythmically with the girl's breath. He probed with his fingers and found it, a hard knot. He looked at the needle and floss nearby. He would be quick, so quick.

There was a knock at the front door.

"Fuck!" he swore, and waited. The person at the door waited.

He cut.

Air swished out of Maddie's lung, bubbling the blood.

Maddie started coughing. He reached into the tiny space and groped around for the tumor.

She was coughing so hard she was choking. Her eyelids were fluttering.

"Mr. Weber?" He heard the voice of that social worker. He pushed harder into the lung with his fingers and found a round hard knob. He pulled on it.

It didn't budge.

Maddie was turning blue. She coughed up blood. Frank's fingers scrambled around in the bloody mess, panicking.

"Oh my God, please don't die," he prayed in a fast, rough whisper. Maddie's eyes were open now, open wide in panic. She thrashed against her restraints.

He had made a horrible mistake.

"Help me!" Frank yelled. He didn't know what to do. He pressed his hand into the cavity he had created, fumbling with his other hand for the needle and thread. He had to get the lung closed back up.

He heard the door handle shaking. Air was whooshing in and out of Maddie's lung as she drew ragged, choking breaths. Frank felt cold all over his body. His hands looked like they belonged to someone else.

"It's locked!"

"Fuck! Fuck!"

Glass broke and the front door opened.

"Where are you?" the social worker shouted.

"In the kitchen! Help me!"

Shelly came hurrying into the kitchen and stopped cold.

"Holy shit, what the fuck have you done?" she shouted.

"Just help me, I have to sew her up!"

"Sew her up?! I'm calling 911!"

"No! They won't help her. Only I can help her. Put pressure here, now!" He grabbed Shelly's hand with his bloody one and drew it to the little girl's side, then fumbled for the threaded needle.

Shelly put pressure on the wound and looked at the white face of the little girl, spotted with blood as she gasped for breath.

With her free hand, she got out her phone and dialed 911.

"911, What is your emergency?"

Shelly didn't even know how to describe what was happening.

"I have an injured child in need of immediate medical attention. She is choking and bleeding profusely."

"What is your location?"

She told them. Frank shoved her to the side and began stitching. The flow of blood did not stop, and the child continued her gasping and coughing. Her eyes rolled around in her head in confusion and fear. Shelly went to her head.

"You're going to be okay, sweetheart, I've got you."

Maddie made a wet, gurgling sound and passed back out.

"I don't know how to do this! Do you know how to sew? Fuck! I thought I could do this!"

"You have lost your fucking mind!" Shelly screamed. "What have you done to this child?" The child in front of her was dying. Her mind flew back to her brother, bleeding from the head on the floor of the kitchen, but she forced herself back to the present.

"Get out of the way!" She ripped the needle from Frank's hand and peered into the broad slit he had left in Maddie's chest. He had made several large, sloppy stitches that were doing nothing to prevent the air from whistling in and out of the sucking wound. She wasn't going to be able to sew this up. With her fingers, she pinched the sides of the incision together and held them.

"Get her on her side! She's choking on her own blood!"

Frank scrambled to untie his daughter, then turned her. She coughed out a clot of blood and took a ragged gasp. Shelly could feel air trickling through her fingers, but the lung began to re-inflate. She heard sirens, finally.

Frank was cradling his daughter's head, crying.

"I didn't get it out. I felt it, but I couldn't get it out."

"Get what out?"

"The tumor."

"What tumor?"

"You don't feel a tumor in there?"

All Shelly felt was soft tissue and slick blood.

Chapter Twenty-Seven

The paramedics made Shelly keep her hand in the wound and loaded her into the rig alongside Maddie. They put in an IV and gave the child morphine. She was wailing loudly between gurgling coughs.

After a few moments, the child quieted, her head lolling to the side.

Frank attempted to push his way into the back of the ambulance.

The paramedic, the same young Black woman who had visited before, looked at Shelly.

"No," Shelly said. "We need the police. He did this."

The paramedic barred his way. "They're on their way," she told Shelly.

"I need to be with her!" Frank shouted.

"You need to wait here," the paramedic said. "Your daughter needs medical care, and right now you are delaying it."

Frank slumped and stepped back off of the vehicle. A police car rolled up behind him, lights flashing. Shelly craned her neck to see which officer it was.

Sinclair. She wanted to tell him to be gentle with the man, that he had lost his mind, but the ambulance was already pulling away.

Chapter Twenty-Eight

Frank stood quietly, letting the officer snap his hands into the cuffs, then bending to enter the back of the police car. The engine rumbled as they took off in the direction of the jail. Frank closed his eyes. All he could see was Maddie's face flecked with blood, her eyes rolling back in her head. He did that. He had hurt his child.

But now, they would find the tumor. They would have to look at her lungs, to repair the cut. They would see what he saw. They would remove the tumor.

He had done the right thing, he told himself. It was his job. He had let his mother waste away into a fragile skeleton wrapped in skin, watched her die gasping in pain, but he had saved Maddie. He had saved her.

Tisha would understand, he told himself. She would have to. She wasn't there, and he was. He did what he had to do.

"Can I call my wife when we get there?" he asked. "I get one phone call, right?"

Sinclair grunted. Then, eyeing Frank in the rearview mirror, he grumbled, "Just out of curiosity, what are you going to tell her? That you carved your daughter up on the kitchen table like the Christmas ham?"

"I didn't–. She was–." Frank didn't know what to say. And he didn't know what he would tell Tisha. Seen through the officer's eyes, he could see it looked like he had lost his mind. Maybe he had.

"She's going to get help now," he told Officer Sinclair. "They'll have to help her."

Sinclair gave a harsh little laugh. "Hopefully not like you did," he said.

Chapter Twenty-Nine

Shelly got off the phone with Mae, who was pissed that she wasn't going to get her form, pissed that there had been another emergency on Shelly's watch, and overall just pissed. But Shelly pushed that from her mind and watched the little girl in the bed. The child was watching television with a dull look on her face, breathing raggedly and clearly in pain despite the loads of narcotics they had pumped into her.

A doctor came in, listened to her breathing.

"Her dad said she had a tumor," Shelly said.

"We've looked again," the doctor said. He was a youngish white man with sandy blond hair. "There's no tumor. We've confirmed a respiratory infection and started her on a stronger course of antibiotics. The infection would have cleared up in a couple of days. Obviously this complicates things."

"Where's my Daddy?" Maddie asked, looking at the doctor and then at Shelly.

"He's busy right now," Shelly said, not sure what else to say. Frank was sitting in jail. "You can talk to him soon if you want to." The call would probably be up to her, and she decided she would allow it. One more thing to piss Mae off, most likely, but she had seen the look in Frank's eyes. He had been frantic to save his daughter.

Maddie shook her head 'No,' and refocused her eyes on the television.

Shelly thanked the voice in her head for pushing her to check on the family. How many times had she medicated that voice out of existence? How many times had the pills come first? How many children had she not helped?

Shelly's phone rang. It was Maddie's mother. Shelly had left her a message once the police got her number from Frank.

"What the hell happened? Is Maddie okay? Who are you?"

Shelly told her in as few words as possible. Her husband had attempted surgery on her daughter, he was in jail, and Maddie was okay. She lied on that part. This child wasn't going to be okay for a long time; Shelly could tell from her vacant stare. She knew that look. She had lived that look. But she was alive. That was something.

"Drive carefully," she told the woman, who now couldn't stop crying. "I've got her until you get here."

About Ruth Anna Evans

RUTH ANNA EVANS

Ruth Anna Evans is a writer of short horror fiction, an anthologizer, and a cover designer who lives in the heart of all that is sinister: the American Midwest. She has been composing prose of all types since childhood but finds something truly delightful in putting her nightmares on the page. She has published OH FUCK OH FUCK IT HURTS: A Collection of Medical Horror, as well as a couple of novellas, an anthology (OOZE: Little Bursts of Body Horror), and a whole bunch of short stories and novelettes. Follow Ruth Anna on Twitter @ruthannaevans, on Facebook at Ruth Anna Evans, on Instagram at ruthannaevanshorror, or at her website www.ruthannaevans.com for updates on her work.

Also By Ruth Anna Evans

Novellas
Do Not Go In That House
Hungry (available exclusively on godless.com)
What Did Not Die

Anthologies/Collections
No One Can Help You:
Tales of Lost Children and Other Nightmares

RUTH ANNA EVANS

OOZE: Little Bursts of Body Horror
OH FUCK OH FUCK IT HURTS: A Collection of Medical Horror

www.ruthannaevans.com